Fred and Pete at the Beach

by Cynthia Nugent

ORCA BOOK PUBLISHERS

To Ron, for rescuing Fred and Pete from the SPCA.
And to his mother, who sent him directions from Heaven.

Library and Archives Canada Cataloguing in Publication

Nugent, Cynthia, 1954-
Fred and Pete at the beach / Cynthia Nugent.

ISBN 978-1-55469-126-5

I. Title.
PS8627.U34F74 2009   jC813'.6   C2009-901666-4

Summary: A humorous story about two dogs determined to find their own way to the beach.

First published in the United States, 2009
Library of Congress Control Number: 2009924735

Orca Book Publishers gratefully acknowledges the support for its publishing programs provided by the following agencies:
the Government of Canada through the Book Publishing Industry Development Program and the Canada Council for the Arts,
and the Province of British Columbia through the BC Arts Council and the Book Publishing Tax Credit.

Cover and interior artwork by Cynthia Nugent
Design by Teresa Bubela
Author photo by Noel MacDonald

ORCA BOOK PUBLISHERS
PO BOX 5626, STN. B
VICTORIA, BC CANADA
V8R 6S4

ORCA BOOK PUBLISHERS
PO BOX 468
CUSTER, WA USA
98240-0468

www.orcabook.com
Printed and bound in Canada.

12 11 10 09 • 4 3 2 1

"You can whimper and whine all you want, but you aren't coming to the beach with me today," Ron said to Fred and Pete.

Fred and Pete watched Ron carry a scrumptious-smelling picnic basket to the car. He placed it on the back seat, next to the beach blanket and their well-chewed Frisbee.

Ron frowned. "And there'll be no Frisbee for you today either," he said, tossing a book onto the front seat.

As Ron backed the car down the driveway, Pete toddled alongside the fence. "Take us with you! Please take us with you," he pleaded.

"Stop begging," Fred said. "You're embarrassing yourself."

Pete flopped down on the grass. "I want to go to the beach. Why, oh why, can't we go too?"

"Because you dragged the garbage all over the kitchen floor," said Fred.

"Did I?" Pete looked confused. Then he groaned and put his head on his paws. "I did, didn't I. What was I thinking?"

"Do now, think later—that's you," said Fred.

"It's such a perfect day for the beach," moaned Pete. "I was looking forward to paddling in the water and digging in the sand. My nose is ready to sniff for fish. I want to bark at crabs and dig a cool hole under a shady tree to lie in."

"Well, don't dig a hole here or we'll really be in trouble," said Fred.

"I know!" cried Pete, leaping up. "Let's walk to the beach."

Fred shook his head. "Oh no, it's too far."

"I wish I had a car," said Pete.

"Don't be silly," said Fred. "You don't know how to drive."

Across the street, a mail truck drove up. The driver got out to deliver a package.

"Look, it's Mike," Pete said.

The dogs ran to the gate, barking and wagging their tails, but Mike didn't turn around to say hello like he usually did.

Pete stopped barking. "Hey, Fred, we can get a ride to the beach in Mike's mail truck! He's our friend."

"Not a close friend," said Fred, squinting through the fence.

But Pete was already wiggling and grunting and squeezing himself under the gate. He trundled across the street and climbed into the truck.

"Wait!" called Fred as he slid under the gate and hurried after him.

It was dark in the truck. Fred saw a shadow move at the back. The shadow was shaped like Pete.

"Please come out, Pete," Fred called nervously.

Suddenly the driver slid behind the wheel and started the engine. The truck surged forward and sped off down the road. Fred tumbled backward. He landed on a mail sack beside Pete.

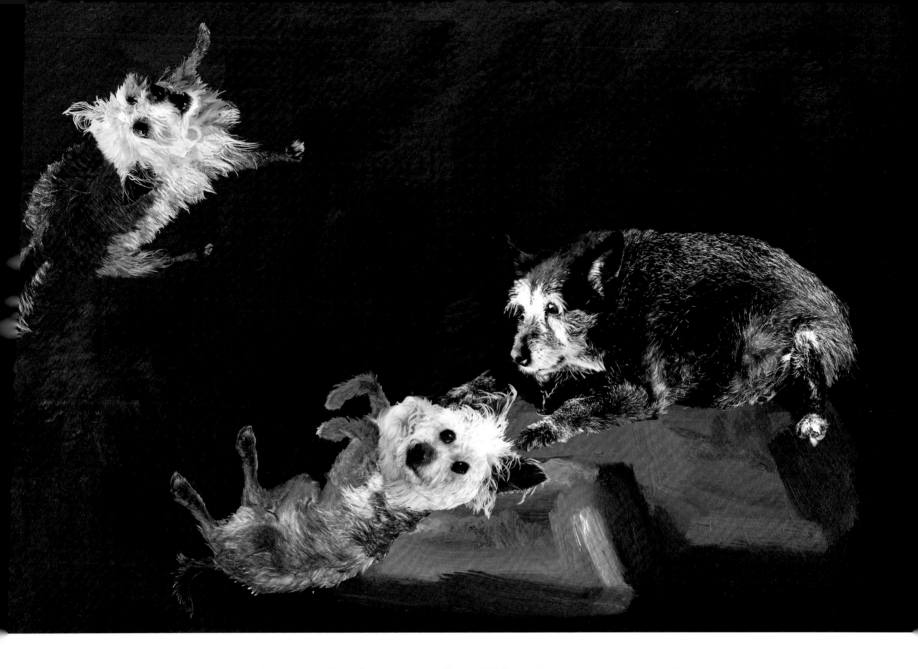

"Hi, Fred. Isn't this fun?" asked Pete. "We'll be there in no time."

"I suppose so," said Fred. "But won't Ron be mad at us?"

"Don't worry, he's never mad for long," said Pete. "Isn't Mike nice to drive us?"

Fred looked up at the man driving the truck and gasped. "Pete! That's not Mike!"

The mail truck zipped along so fast and turned so many corners that Fred and Pete got dizzy. Finally it lurched to a stop. The driver turned to reach for his mailbag. "Hey, what are you dogs doing in my truck? Out!"

Fred and Pete watched the truck drive away.

"Now what?" said Fred. "We don't even know where we are. Trying to find the beach on our own was a dumb idea."

"Don't say that. We'll find the beach, you'll see," said Pete.

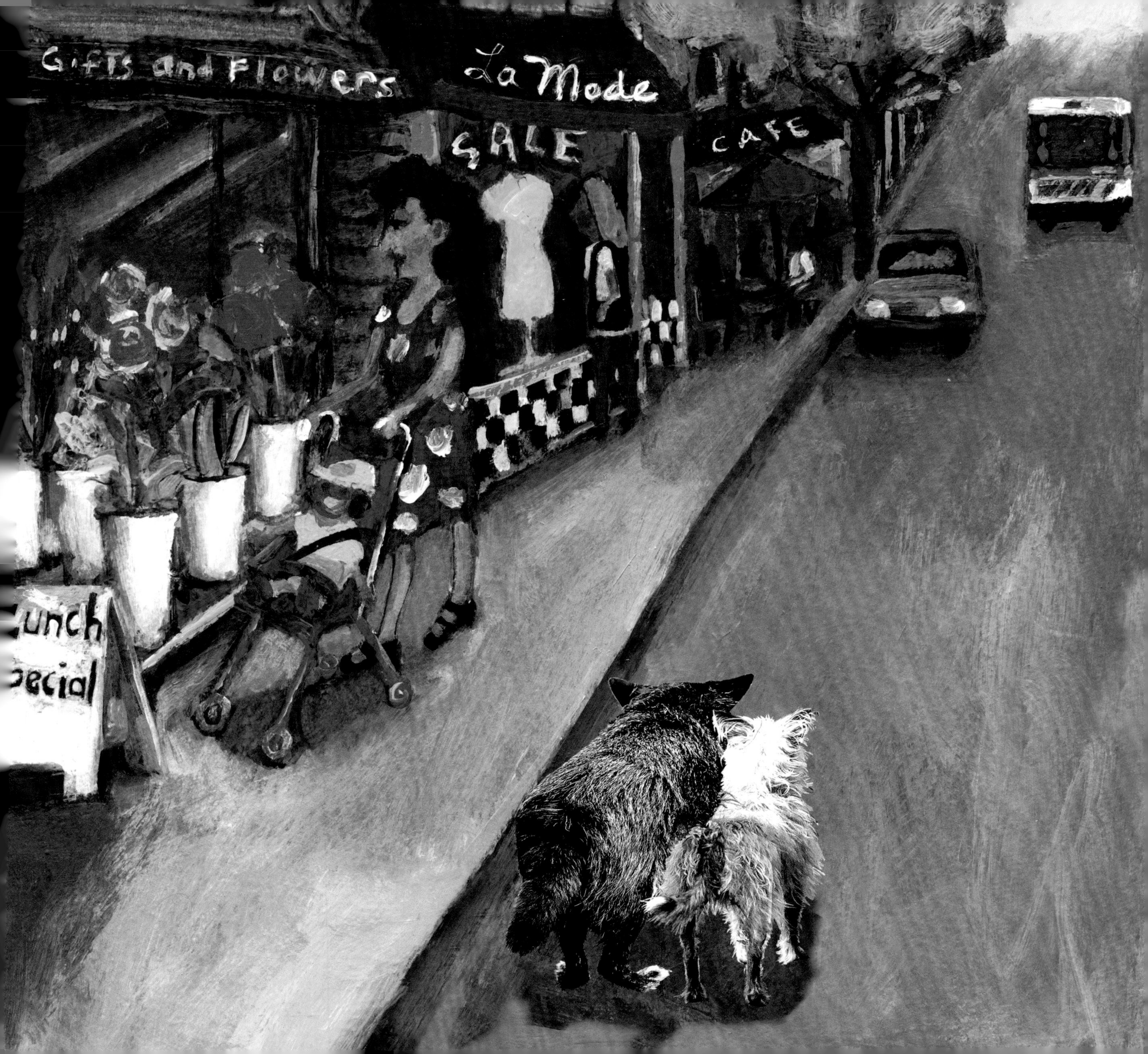
Gifts and Flowers
La Mode
SALE
CAFE
unch
ecial

"Yoo-hoo," called a woman riding a bicycle. She pulled up to the curb to talk to her friend. Attached to the back of her bike was a little yellow trailer.

"Look at her," whispered Pete. "She's wearing sunglasses and has sunscreen goop on her nose. She must be going to the beach. Let's go with her. We can ride in this yellow bubble!"

Fred pushed his head through the trailer flap. "Pete, there's a baby in here."

Pete looked inside. "Don't worry, Fred. It's only a small baby. There's plenty of room for us," he said and hopped in.

"See you soon," the woman called to her friend.
Fred scrambled in after Pete just as the bubble began to move.

The baby looked at Fred, and his bottom lip quivered.

"Stop looking so worried," said Pete. "You're scaring the baby."

Fred made his happy face and gently wagged his tail. The baby smiled.

"I'm getting hungry," said Pete. "I wonder how long it will be before we get to the beach."

"By the time we get to the beach, there'll be nothing left in the picnic basket," grumbled Fred.

"Oh, Fred, you always think things will go wrong."

"They usually do," said Fred.

The bike sped down busy streets and shady streets, down winding lanes and over speed bumps, until it turned a corner and rocked to a stop. A big face appeared in the bubble's opening. Fred and Pete yelped, and the woman squealed, "Eek! Dogs! Get out!"

Fred and Pete toppled out of the bubble and onto the sidewalk. As the woman wheeled her bike away, she gave the dogs a dirty look.

"This is terrible!" said Fred. "We're lost, everyone's yelling at us and I'm hungry. We'll never get to the beach. I want to go home."

"Don't fret, Fred. We'll find the beach. I just know it's nearby." Pete sniffed the air. "I smell the ocean! It is close!"

"Well, it can't be that close. I can't smell anything," said Fred. He sat down on the sidewalk. "This is impossible."

"Nothing is impossible, Fred!"

Just then, a bus pulled up. Many of the people boarding the bus wore
sunglasses and carried picnic baskets, beach umbrellas and blankets.

"Look at those people, Fred. This bus must be going to the beach.
Can't you smell the suntan lotion? Hurry, let's jump on!"
"That's what you said about the mail truck and the bicycle," said Fred.

But Pete wasn't listening. He had already scooted onto the
bus through the rear door. Fred sighed and followed after him.

Pete had found a window seat at the back of the bus.
Fred hopped up beside him.

"Isn't this perfect?" asked Pete.

"We'll see," said Fred.

The bus wound down a steep hill. The salty seaside smell grew so strong even Fred started to get excited.

The two dogs tumbled off the bus at the next stop and ran toward the water. The sand was warm under their paws. The breeze lifted their fur, carrying the whiff of wet rocks and seaweed, flickering fish and tiny scuttling crabs.

Pete charged along the water's edge, snapping at the foam and barking at the seagulls. Fred sat on the sand. He gazed around at all the families, children and dogs chasing Frisbees.

Pete ran up and shook water all over Fred. "What are you looking at, Fred?"

"That's sad," said Fred. "That person is all by himself. Where's his family?"

Pete followed his gaze. There was Ron, alone on the blanket, reading his book. "That's Ron, Fred! *We're* his family. Come on! Maybe there's some picnic left."

Ron was so happy to see Fred and Pete. He gave them each a sandwich and poured some water into a dish.

"I guess I'll never know how you got here," he said, patting them fondly, "but I'm glad you did."